JEFF WHEELER
MUIRWOOD
coloring book

I0521362

CHARACTERS BY: JEFF WHEELER

COVER ART BY: JULIUS OHTA

ARTWORK BY: JULIUS OHTA

DESIGN BY: Les Dabel & David Campiti

www.glasshousegraphics.com

FOLLOW US ONLINE:
WWW.DABELBROTHERS.COM

Twitter: @DabelBrothers
Facebook: facebook.com/dabelbrothers

DABEL BROTHERS:

Jay Gentry - CEO
Ernst Dabel - President
Les Dabel - V.P. Licensing
Derek Ruiz - Publisher
Patrick Victor - V.P. Sales

Grant Alter - Editor-in-Chief
Dave Lanphear - Creative Director
Gladys Atwell - Marketing Director
Anthony Zicari: - Editor / Sr. Writer

Tips on how to color this Coloring Book:

Thank you for purchasing this Dabel Brothers Coloring Book.

It's one of many Coloring Books we currently have available from your favorite authors, book series, TV shows, Movies, Games, Musician... the list goes on and will continue to grow as we add more amazing Coloring Books to our lineup.

If you enjoyed this Coloring Book please make sure to post your colored pages on our social media and leave us a review. We also encourage you to purchase a copy for your loved ones, as coloring is a great source of stress relief.

Make sure to visit our website DabelBrothers.com for news on upcoming titles and free goodies.

Yours Truly,

Dabel Brothers

1 Always test any markers before you start coloring, using the test page in the back of the book to see if the marker bleeds through or leaves a shadow.

2 If you are using a marker, paint or watercolor pencils. Slip a piece of paper behind the page your are coloring to protect the pages behind from bleed through issues.

3 Have LOTS of fun coloring and always remember, coloring is twice as fun when you are coloring with others. So make sure you have plenty of copies of this book for you and your loved ones :)

Colvin

The Aldermaston

Jon Hunter

Martin Evnissyen

Edmon, Earl of Norris-York

Sheriff Almaguer

Scarseth

Parageis, The Queen Dowager

Aldermaston of Tintern

Hillel Lavender

Marciana Price

Earl of Dieyre

Alluwyn Lleu-Iselin

Duerden Fesit

Aldermaston of Dochte

Kieren Ven

Garen Demont

Muirwood Abbey

Abbey Kitchen

Test Page: